FARGO PUBLIC LIBRARY

T4. AVE.199

by Elizabeth Catanese illustrated by Benedetta Capriotti

MT. OLYMPVS THEME PARK

PANDORA'S PHONE

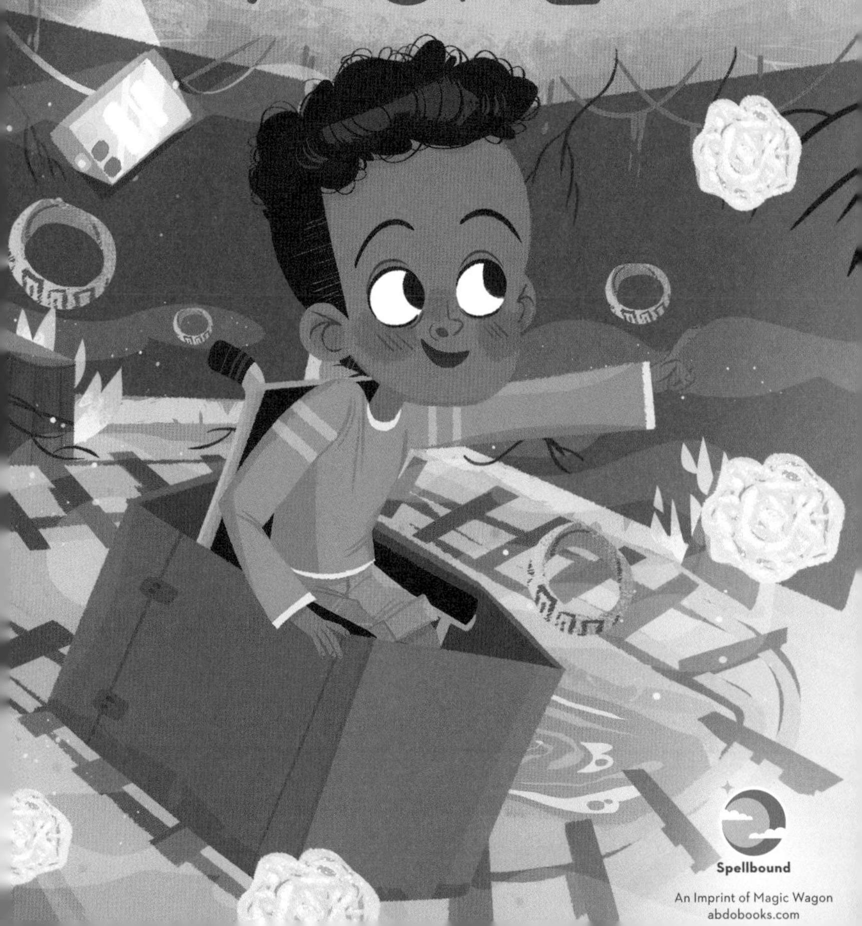

Spellbound
An Imprint of Magic Wagon
abdobooks.com

For Betsy Self Elijah and Micah Elijah, with gratitude for your awesomeness and our friendship. –EC

To Trilly. –BC

abdobooks.com

Published by Magic Wagon, a division of ABDO, PO Box 398166, Minneapolis, Minnesota 55439. Copyright © 2022 by Abdo Consulting Group, Inc. International copyrights reserved in all countries. No part of this book may be reproduced in any form without written permission from the publisher. Spellbound™ is a trademark and logo of Magic Wagon.

Printed in the United States of America, North Mankato, Minnesota.
052021
092021

Written by Elizabeth Catanese
Illustrated by Benedetta Capriotti
Edited by Bridget O'Brien
Art Directed by Laura Graphenteen

Library of Congress Control Number: 2020947933

Publisher's Cataloging-in-Publication Data

Names: Catanese, Elizabeth, author. | Capriotti, Benedetta, illustrator.
Title: Pandora's phone / by Elizabeth Catanese ; illustrated by Benedetta Capriotti.
Description: Minneapolis, Minnesota : Magic Wagon, 2022. | Series: Mt. Olympus theme park
Summary: After getting separated from his brother in the crowds of Mt. Olympus Theme Park, Harvey decides to go on Pandora's box, the only ride available to wheelchair users, but when he finds himself in the middle of the myth, he helps Pandora's creator craft a new character.
Identifiers: ISBN 9781098230395 (lib. bdg.) | ISBN 9781098230951 (ebook) | ISBN 9781098231231 (Read-to-Me ebook)
Subjects: LCSH: Amusement parks--Juvenile fiction. | Mythology, Greek--Juvenile fiction. | People with disabilities--Juvenile fiction. | Pandora (Greek mythological character)--Juvenile fiction. | Amusement rides--Juvenile fiction. | Gods, Greek--Juvenile fiction
Classification: DDC [FIC]--dc23

Table of Contents

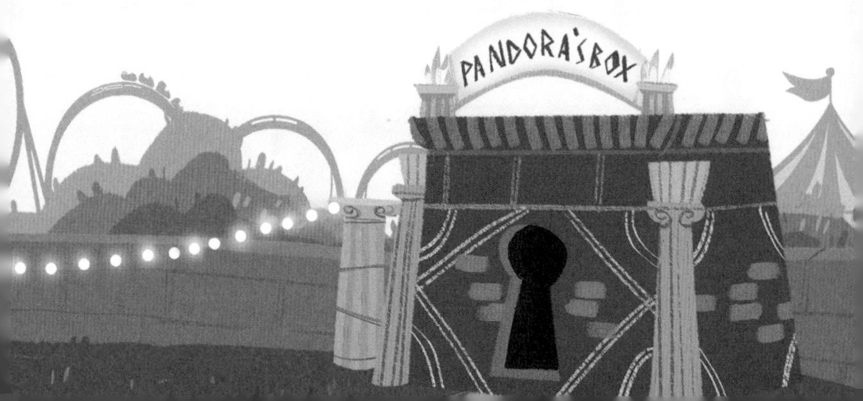
PANDORA'S BOX

Chapter 1

THE VIRTUAL WORLD

"I can't believe Dad got you that Xbox," says Harvey's younger brother, Rob. "Now you're never going to LEAVE the house."

Harvey backs up his wheelchair and hands a controller to his brother. "Wanna play?"

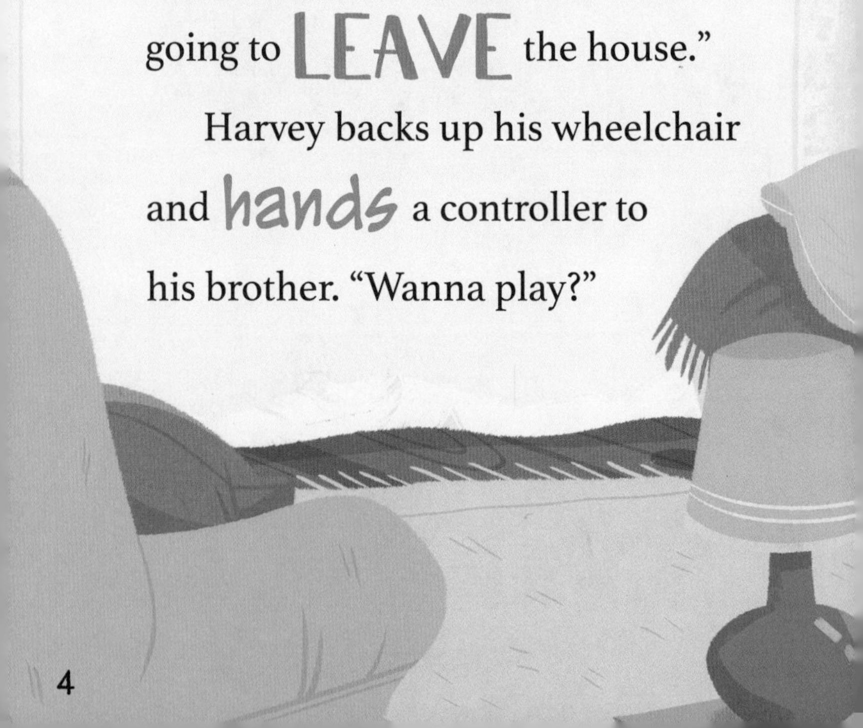

"Dad bought us tickets to Mt. Olympus Theme Park today! REMEMBER?" Rob exclaims.

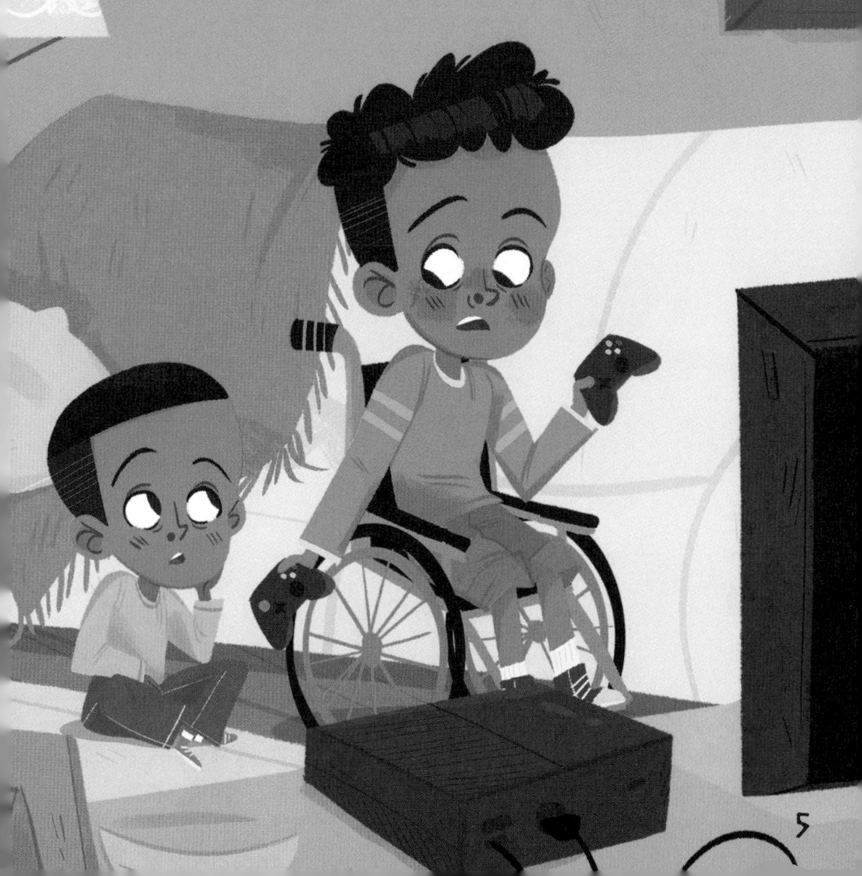

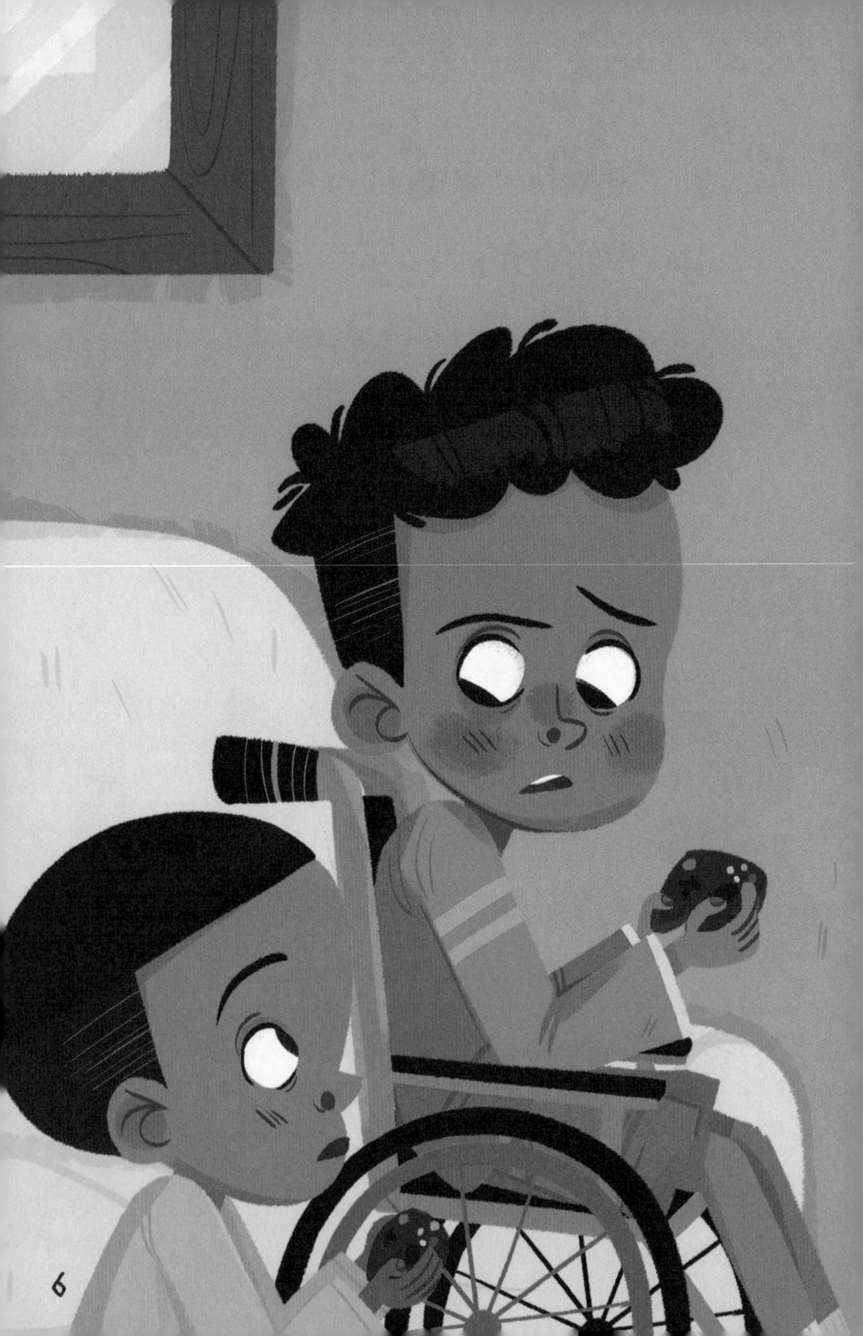

"**UGH**," says Harvey. "Can you go without me?"

The last time they went to Mt. Olympus Theme Park, only **ONE** ride was accessible to wheelchair users. Harvey was *BORED*. Then Rob ran off by himself.

"I'll buy you Fates' Funnel Cake," **whines** Rob.

"Done!" says Harvey. Harvey **REALLY** likes Fates' Funnel Cake.

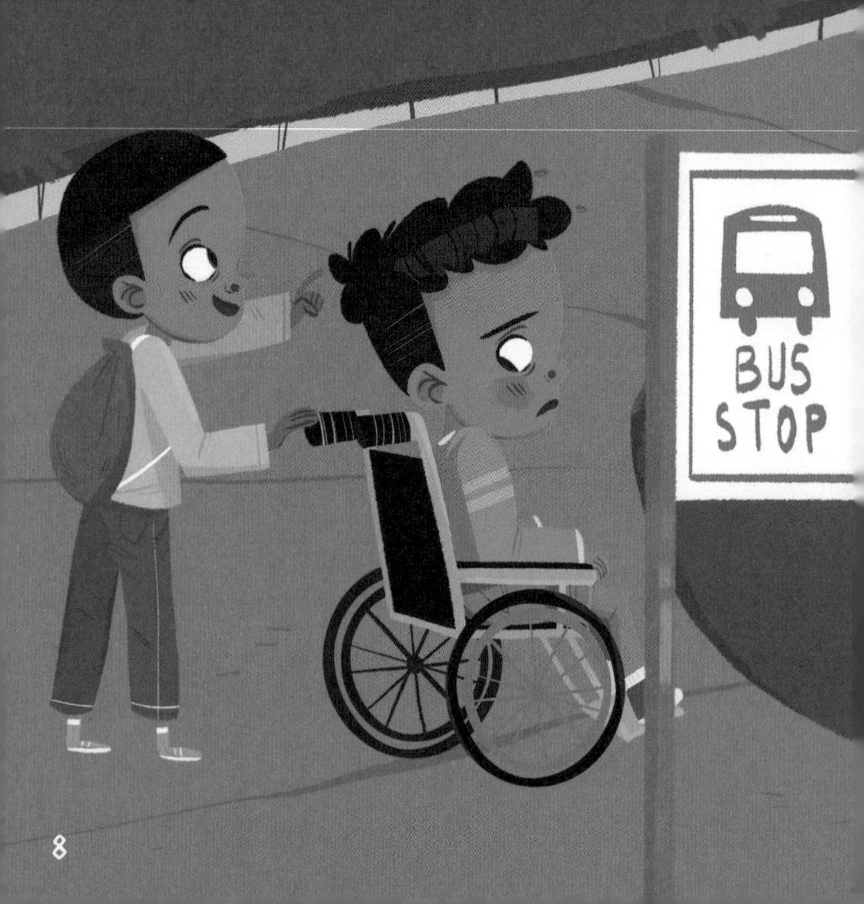
BUS
STOP

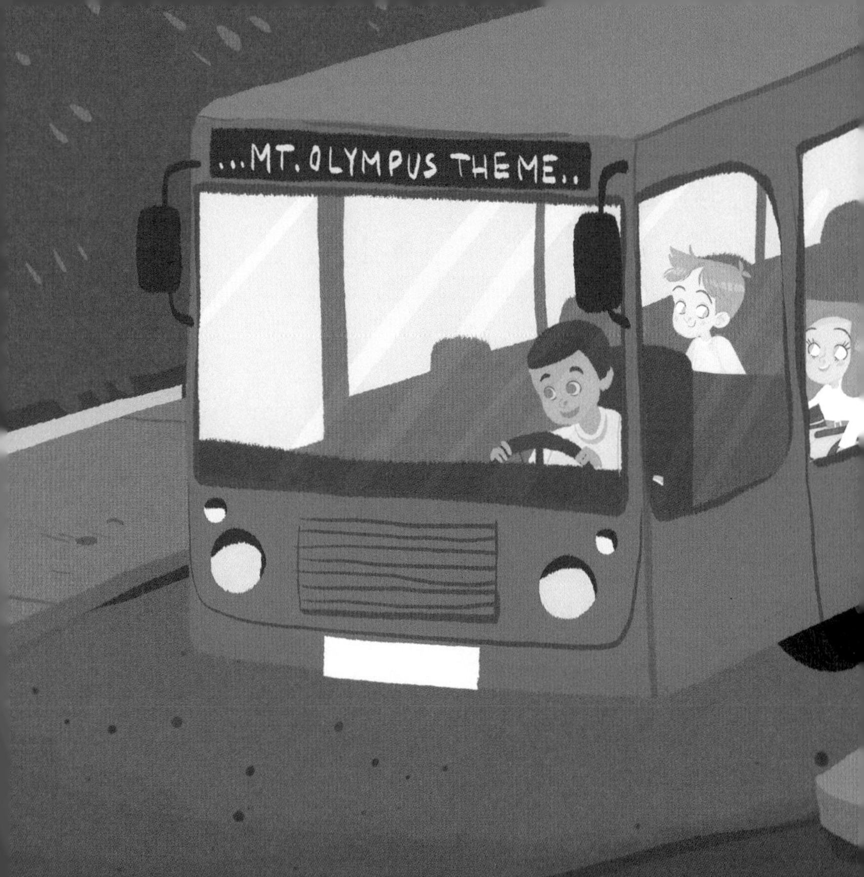
...MT. OLYMPUS THEME..

Mt. Olympus Theme Park is a little far to WALK and roll to, but it's only a ten-minute bus ride away.

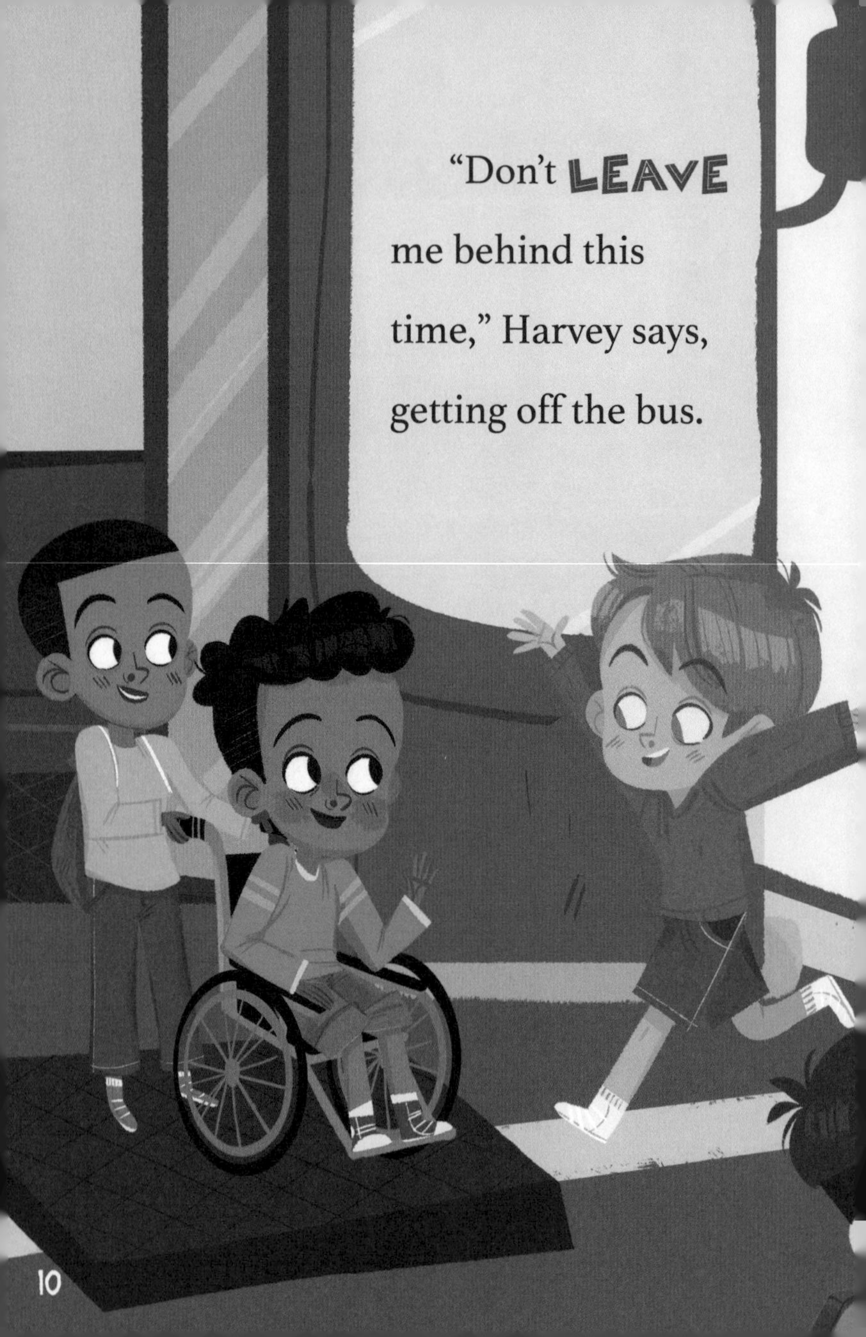

"Don't **LEAVE** me behind this time," Harvey says, getting off the bus.

"Surprise!" Rob's best friend, Micah, runs to greet Rob at the amusement park gates.

Rob's other friend Declan is there too. And Steve. And Juvon. And Temmie. Actually, it seems like all of Rob's friends are at Mt. Olympus Theme Park.

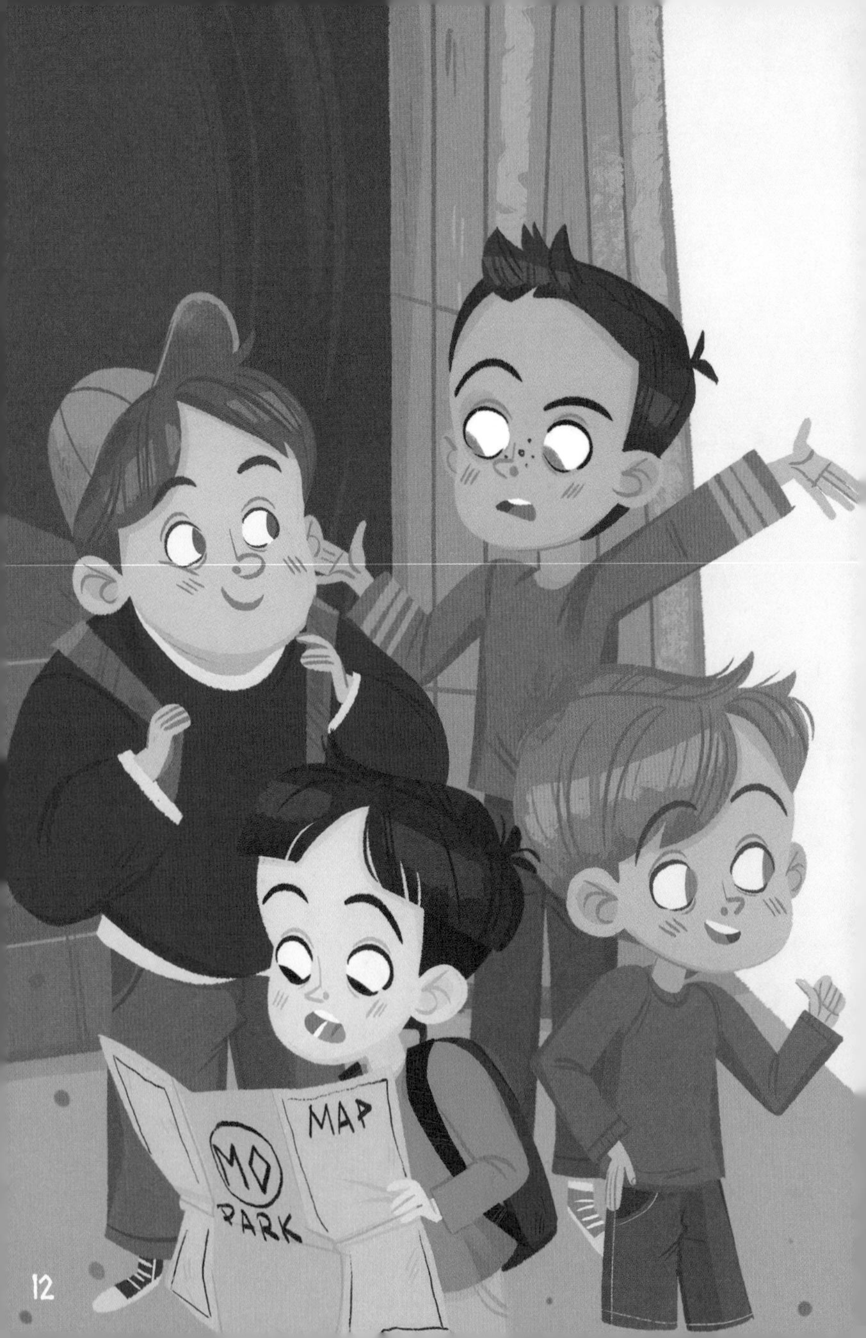
MAP
MO
PARK

"Your dad got us tickets for an early birthday GIFT to you," says Micah to Rob. "Let's go to Zeus Zone! It has a new upside-down roller coaster called Prometheus's Ball of FIRE."

"Fun!" exclaims Rob.

Harvey wheels himself toward Zeus Zone with Rob and his friends. A big crowd of kids dressed as mythological characters cuts him off.

Harvey is on his OWN again. So much for Fates' Funnel Cake!

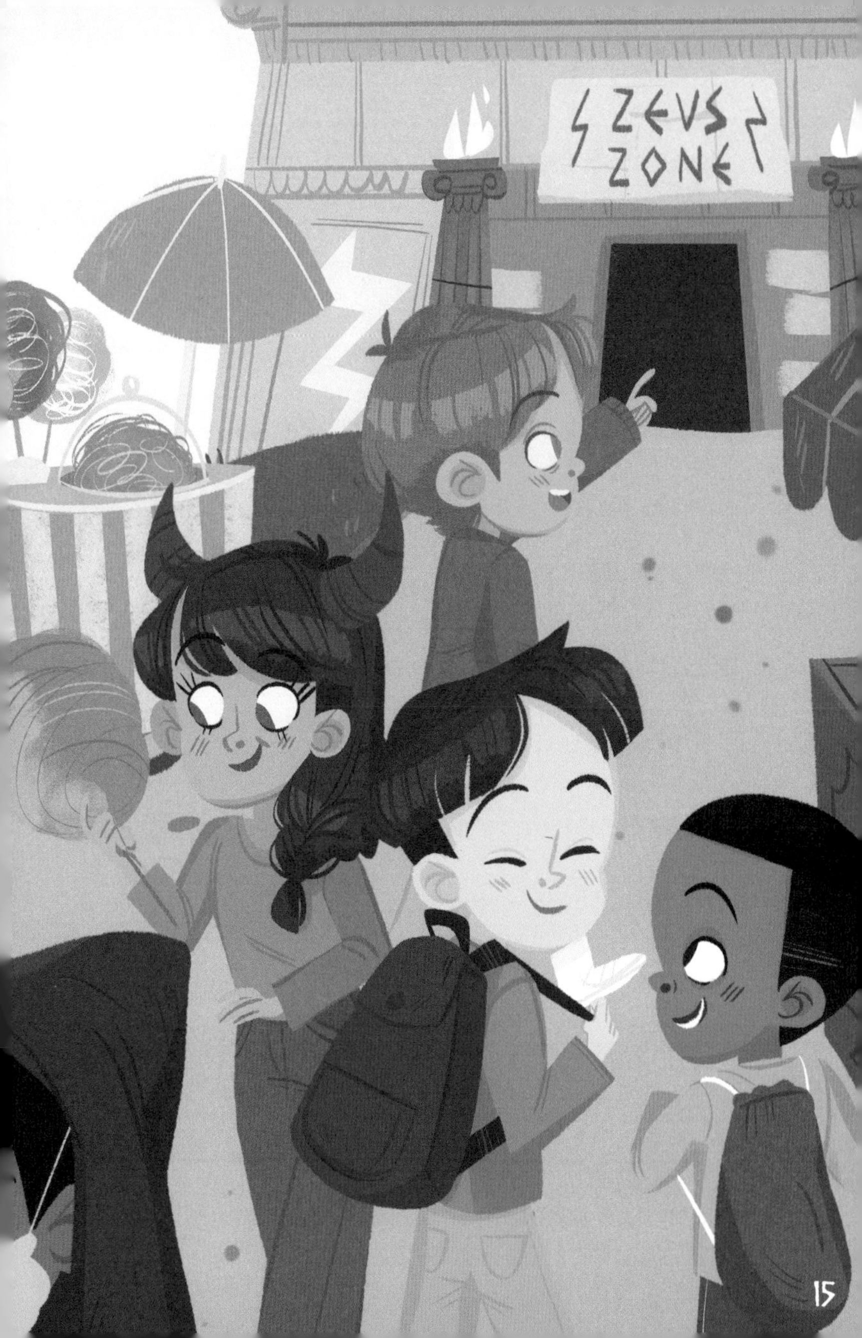
ZEUS ZONE

Chapter 11

AN UNEXPECTED RIDE

Harvey heads toward Zeus Zone. Pandora's Box is the only **ride** that wheelchair users can go on. He might as well try it again.

Harvey arrives at the gold square building with the **FLASHING** *Pandora's Box* sign in purple lights.

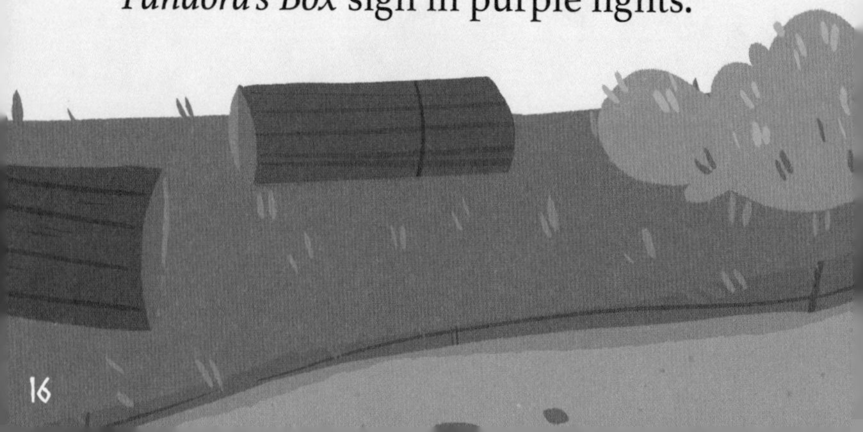

A short guy with wavy yellow hair TAKES his ticket. His name tag says Epimetheus.

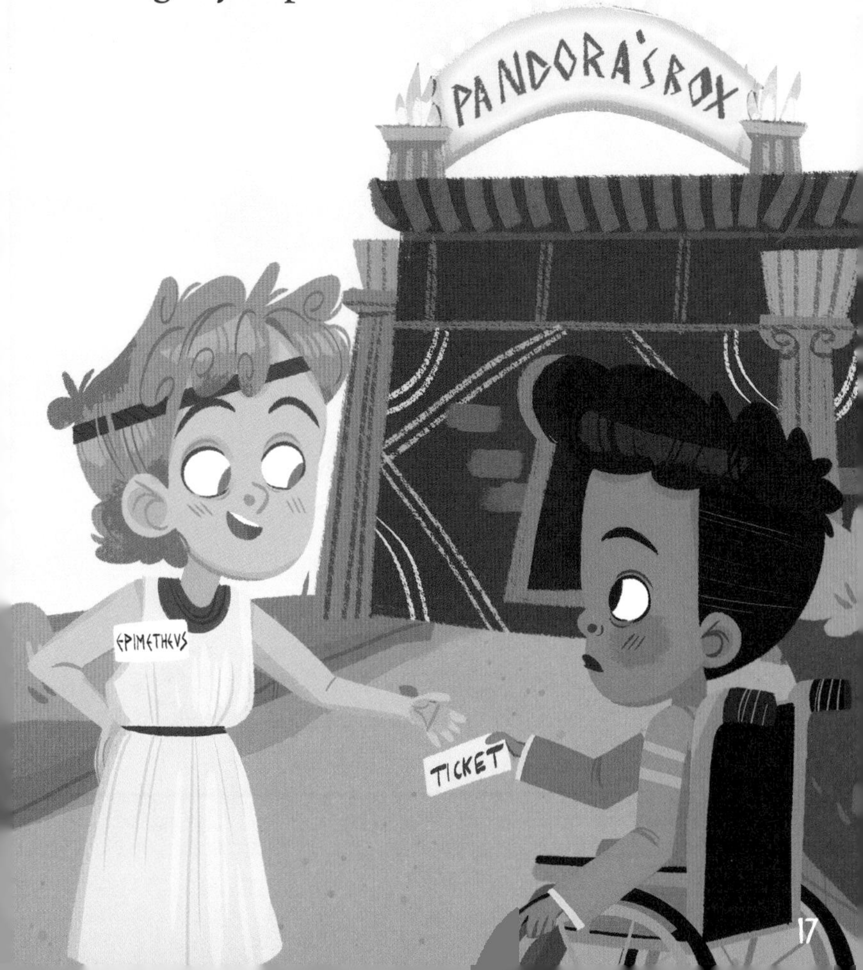
PANDORA'S BOX
EPIMETHEUS
TICKET

"Can you guys try to make this

ride less *BORING*,"

says Harvey.

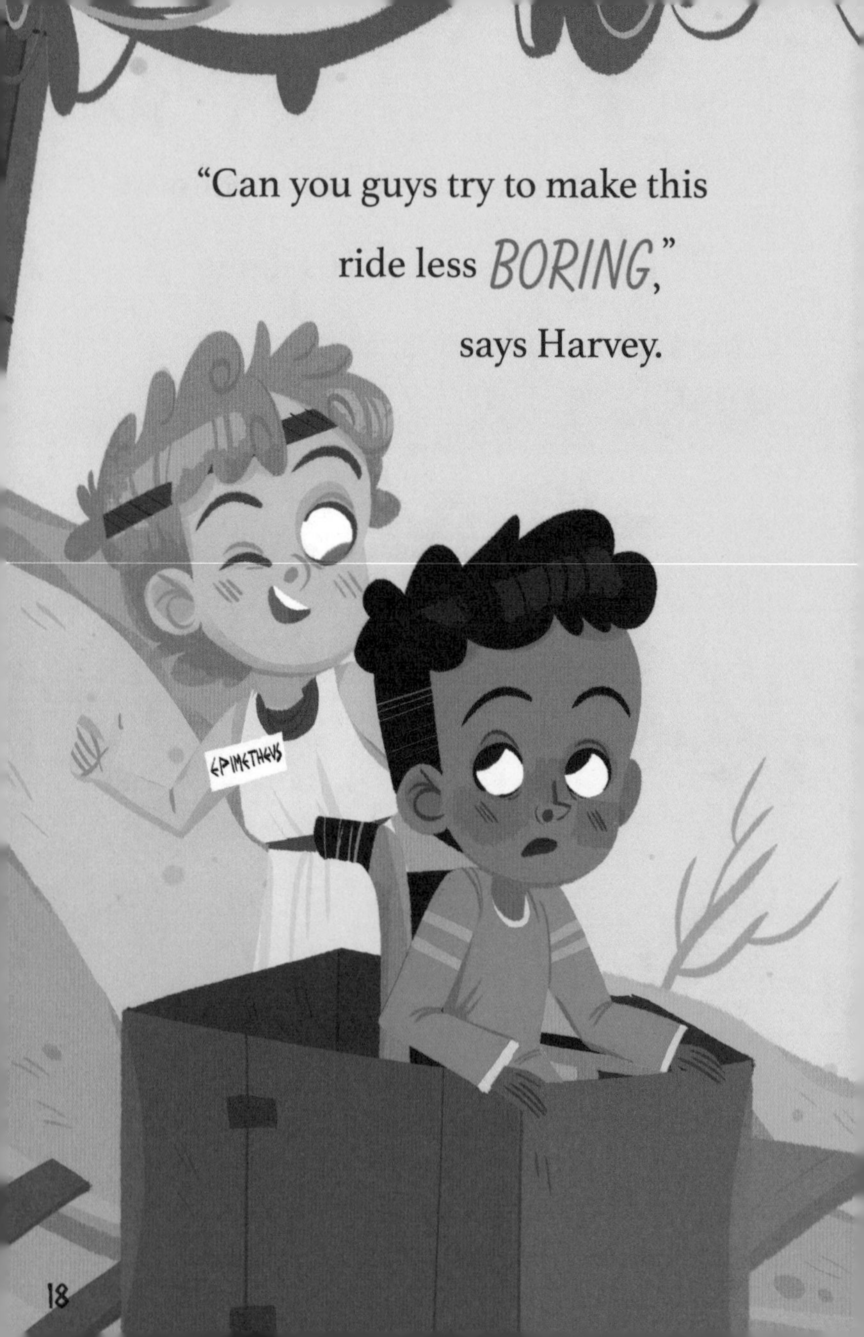
EPIMETHEUS

"Why yes, I can," says Epimetheus. "I have something to SHOW you later."

Harvey doesn't remember Epimetheus from last time. There is something a little SCARY about him. "Are you kidding?" he asks.

"No," Epimetheus says. Harvey rolls up a ramp and into one of the ride's triangle-shaped cars.

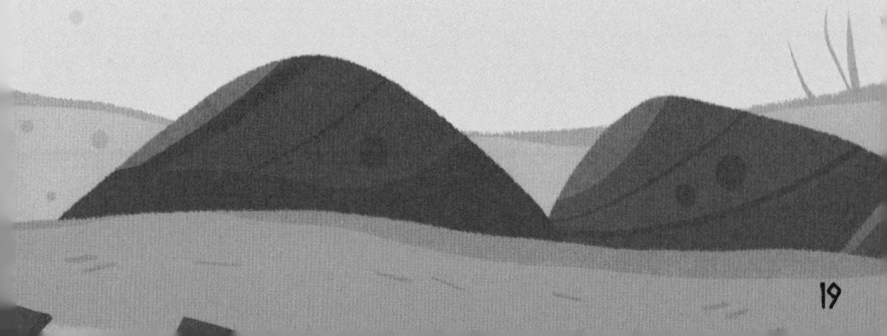

The cars CREEP around TV
screens arranged in a box shape.

The first screen shows an angry
Zeus chucking a LIGHTNING bolt.

The second has Zeus yelling at a
god who holds a cane. "Sculpt
a lady named Pandora!"

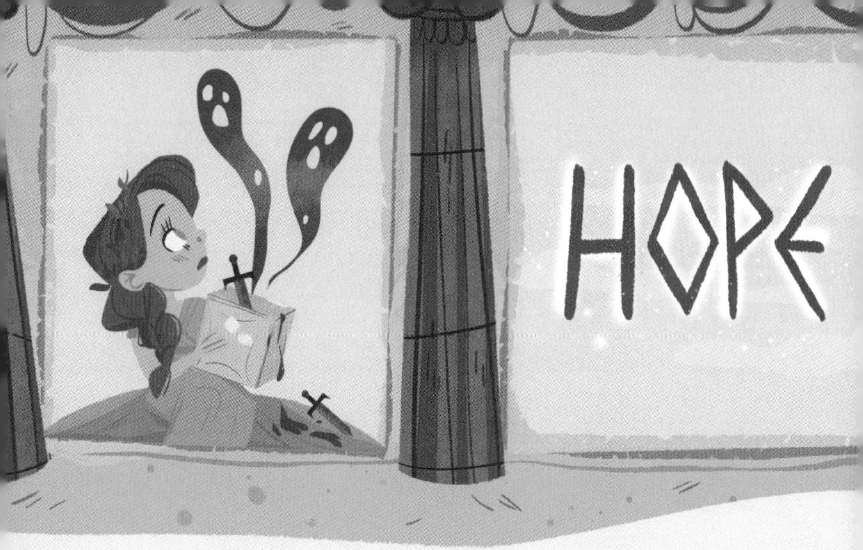
HOPE

The third screen shows Pandora opening a GOLD box. Daggers, blood, and screams FLY out.

On the last screen, the word HOPE flashes. In the myth, hope was the one good thing that came from the box. Ride over. BORING.

When Harvey reaches the second screen, the room goes dark. Everyone **groans**.

Something is strange. Only Harvey is moving. And **FAST**! He's about to **CRASH** into the third screen!

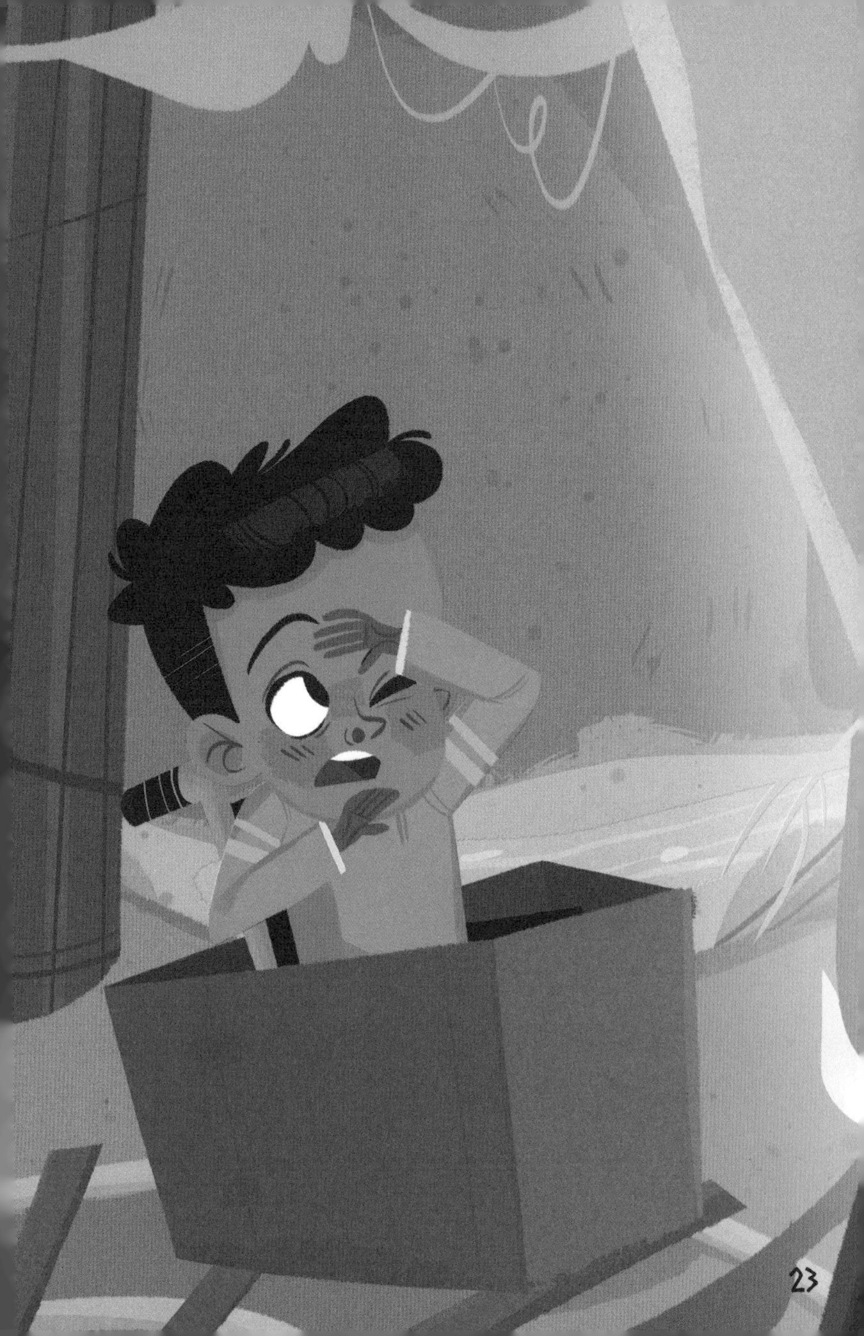

Chapter III

LEONORA

I'm going to die! Harvey thinks.

Then everything **STOPS**.

Harvey is somewhere else.

Epimetheus waves at him. The god

with a **CANE** is there too. Just like

on the ride.

"Where am I?" asks Harvey.

"Ever wonder what's **INSIDE** the box made by the TV screens?" asks Epimetheus.

"Actually, no," says Harvey.

"You're in a Greek myth, and we need your **HELP**."

"I'm Hephaestus," the god with the cane says. "Zeus **BOSSES** me around because I can't walk well. I have to **sculpt** a lady named Pandora to open that."

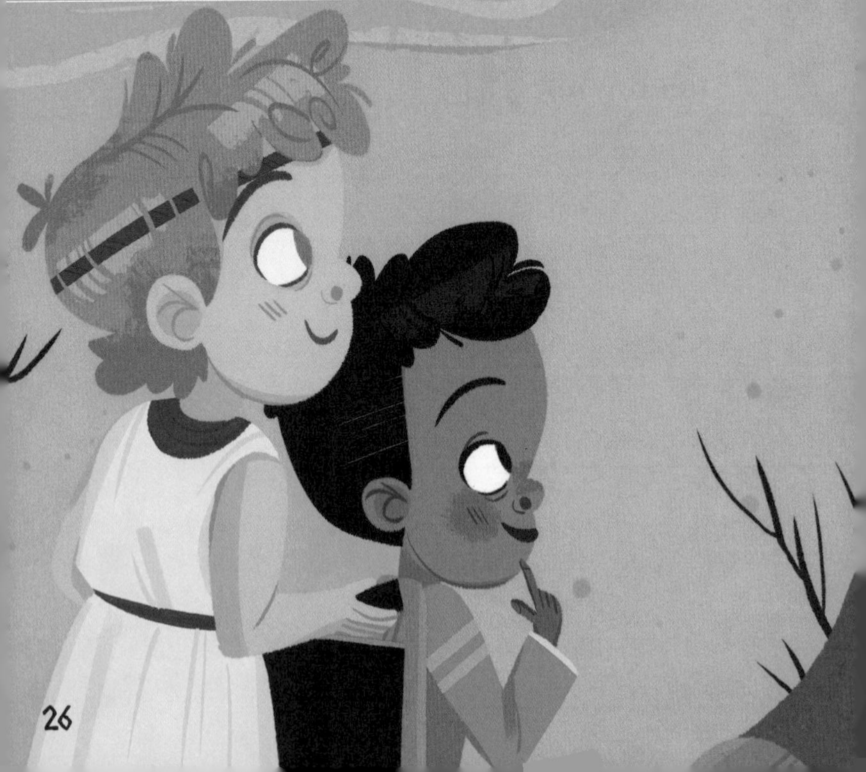

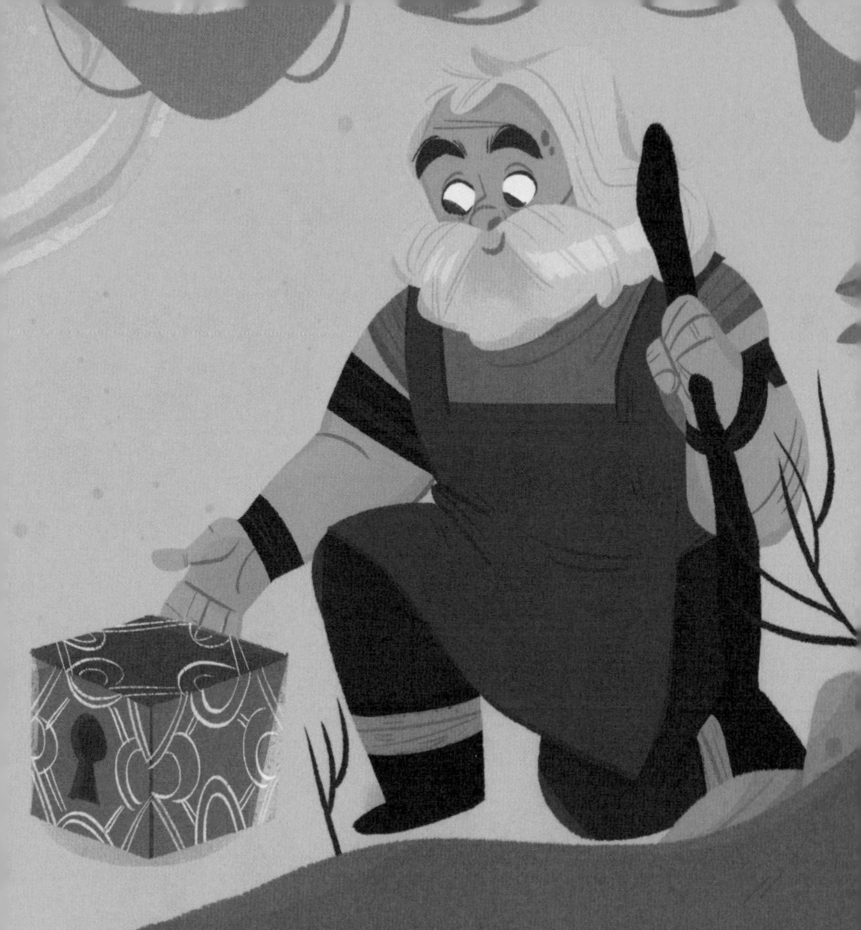

Hephaestus points to a GOLD box on the ground. "But it's going to cause a lot of TROUBLE for everyone."

"I can HELP you make something different," says Harvey.

"We only have clay and FIRE," says Hephaestus.

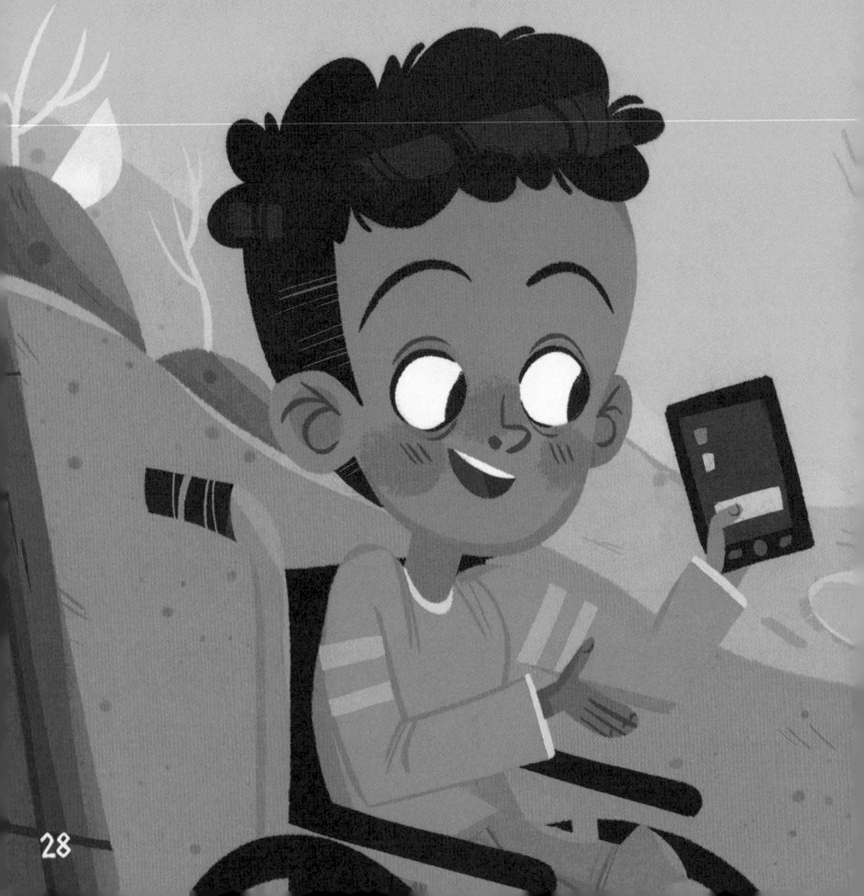

"I have a **smart** phone," says Harvey. "Let's think outside the box. We can design someone *like* Pandora on my phone. Then you can **sculpt** her IRL."

"What's IRL?" asks Epimetheus.

"In real life," says Harvey.

Epimetheus, Harvey, and Hephaestus **design** a new character on an app on Harvey's phone. She looks similar to Pandora.

Harvey **SUGGESTS** that she be a wheelchair user. Epimetheus suggests that she have brown eyes. Once Hephaestus **sculpts** her, Harvey gives her a name.

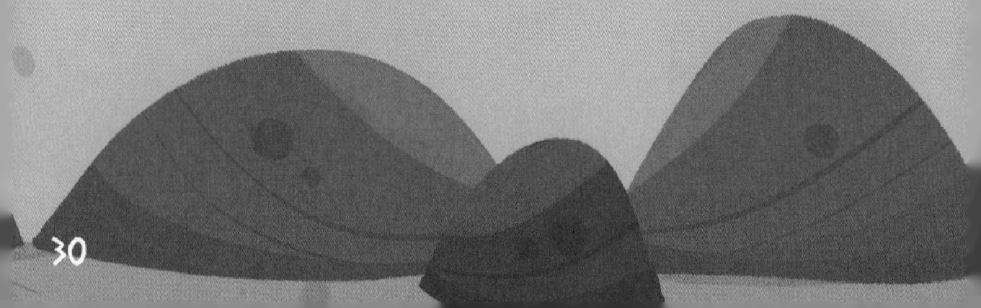

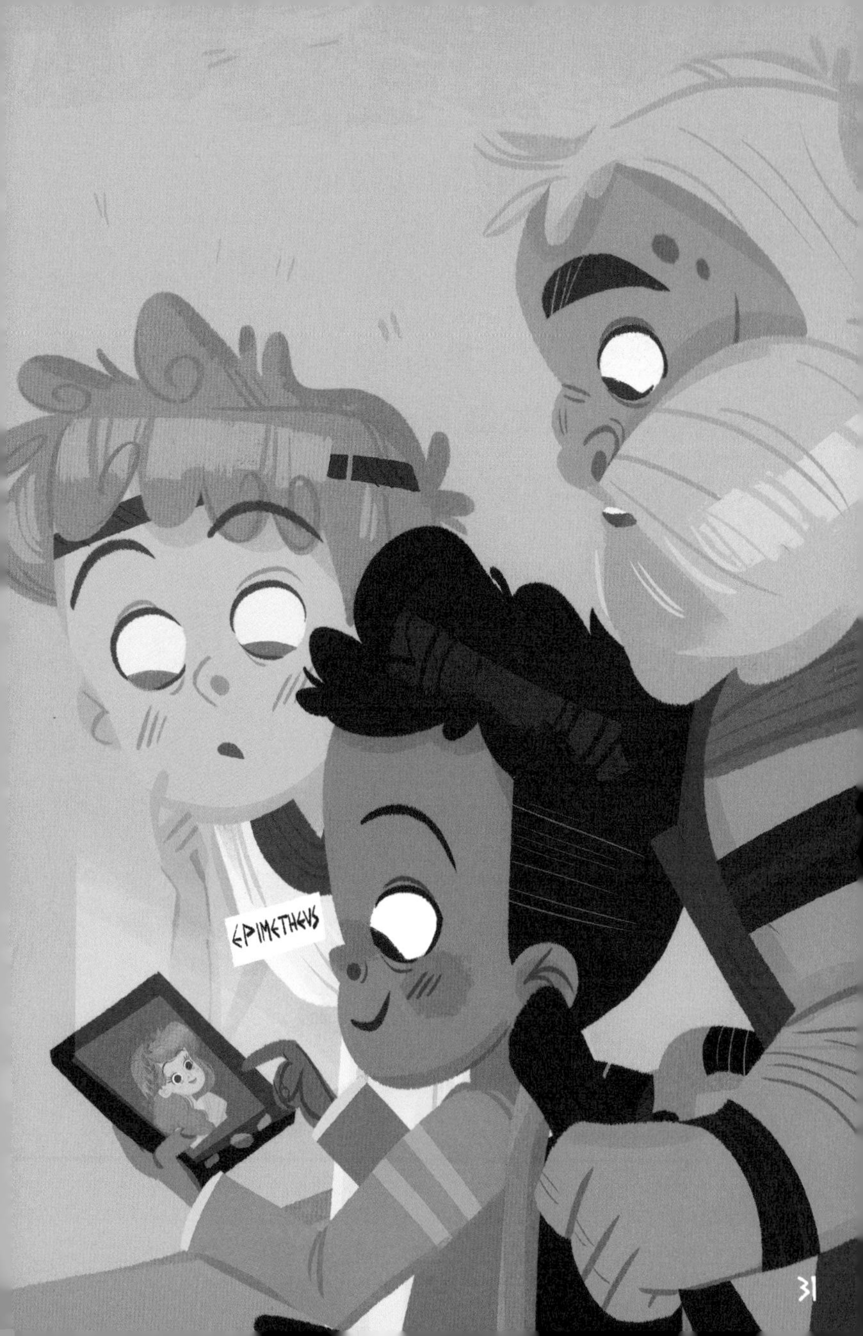
EPIMETHEUS

"Hi, Leonora," says Harvey. "Your job is to **OPEN** this box. But to change the outcome, we're adding this *inclusion* ring. I got it from my school's DREAM club, which is for students with disabilities. I want *everyone* to feel included."

"Sure thing," says Leonora.

WOOSH. Leonora opens the box, and Harvey feels a PUSH forward. He's headed toward a TV screen again!

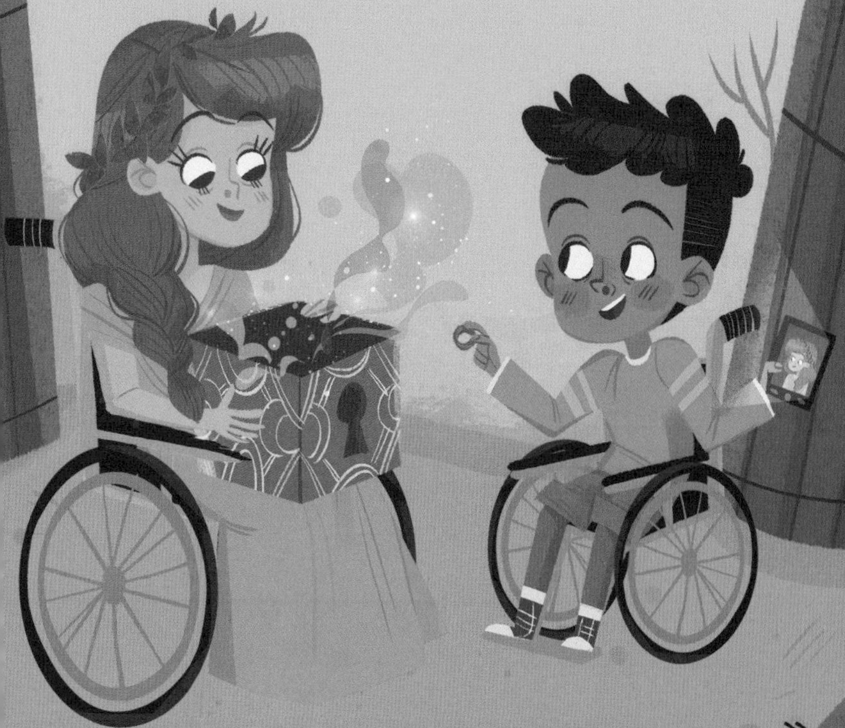

Chapter IV
INCLUSION AT OLYMPUS

SUDDENLY, Harvey is back on the Pandora's Box ride at Mt. Olympus Theme Park. The final screen says *HOPE* and, in gold letters, the word *inclusion*.

HOPE

INCLUSION

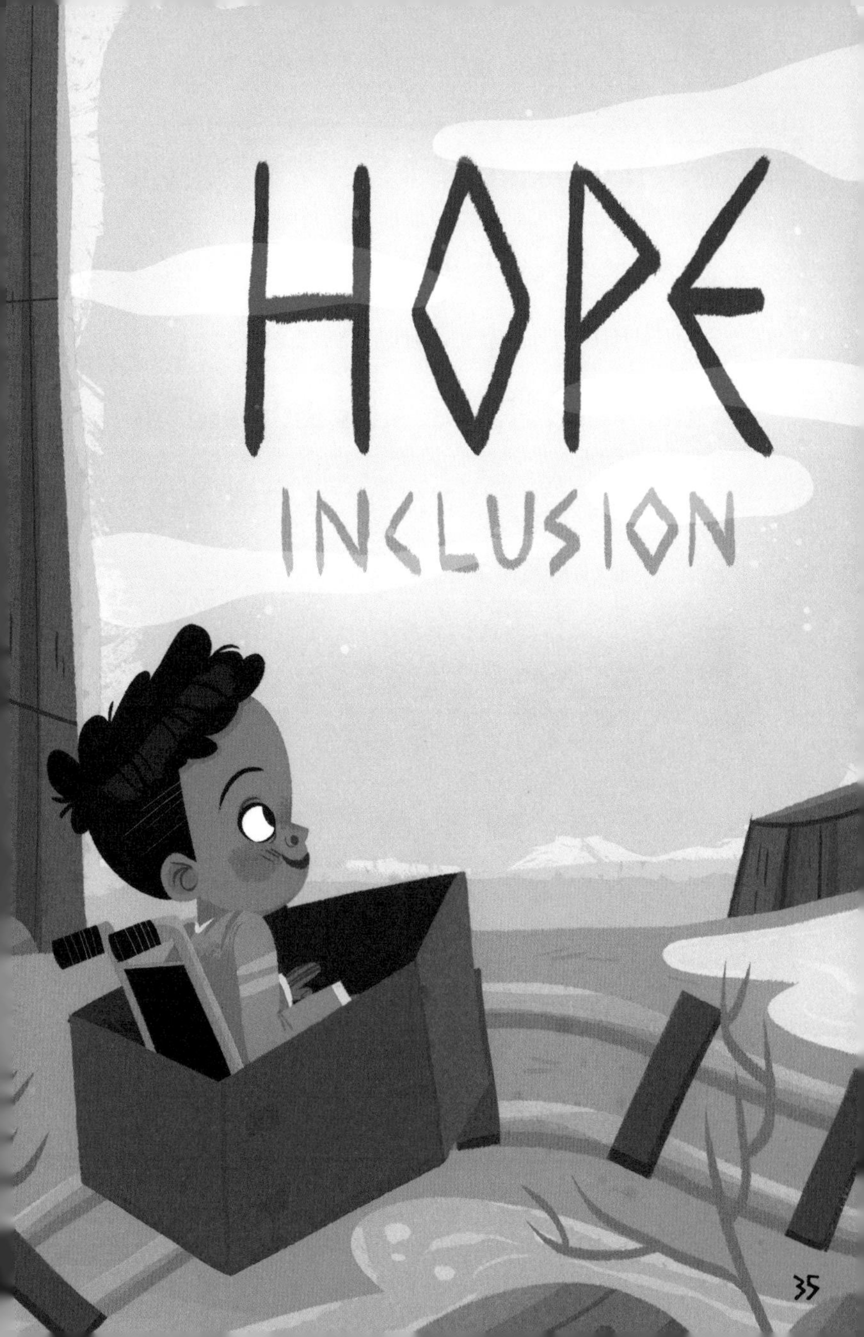

"It worked," whispers Harvey.

"Cool ride," says a kid in a wheelchair as Harvey exits the ride. Then Harvey sees Rob and his friends RUNNING toward him.

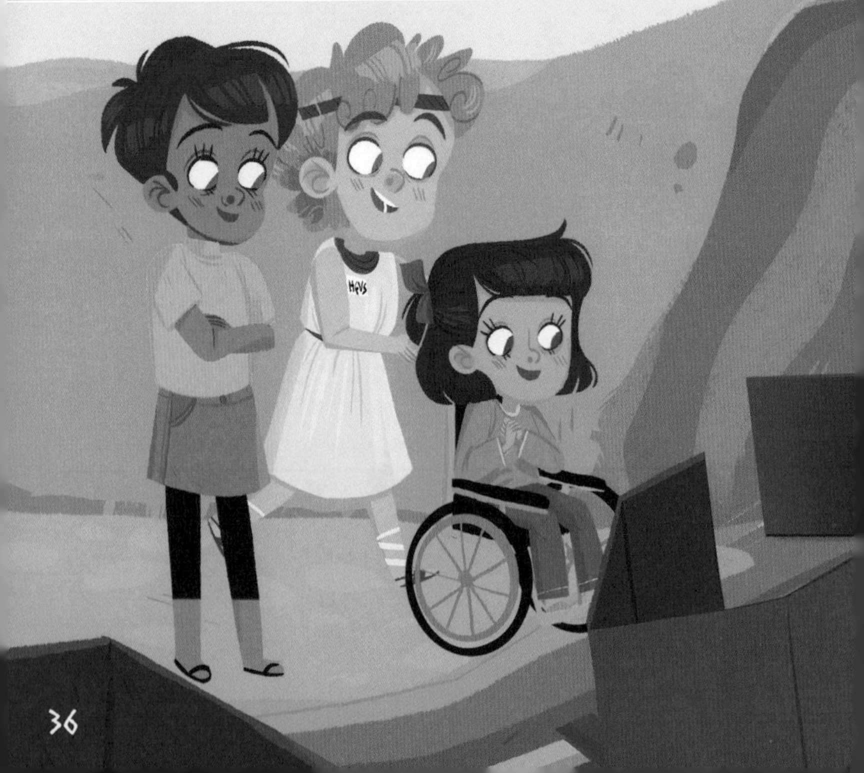
HGVS

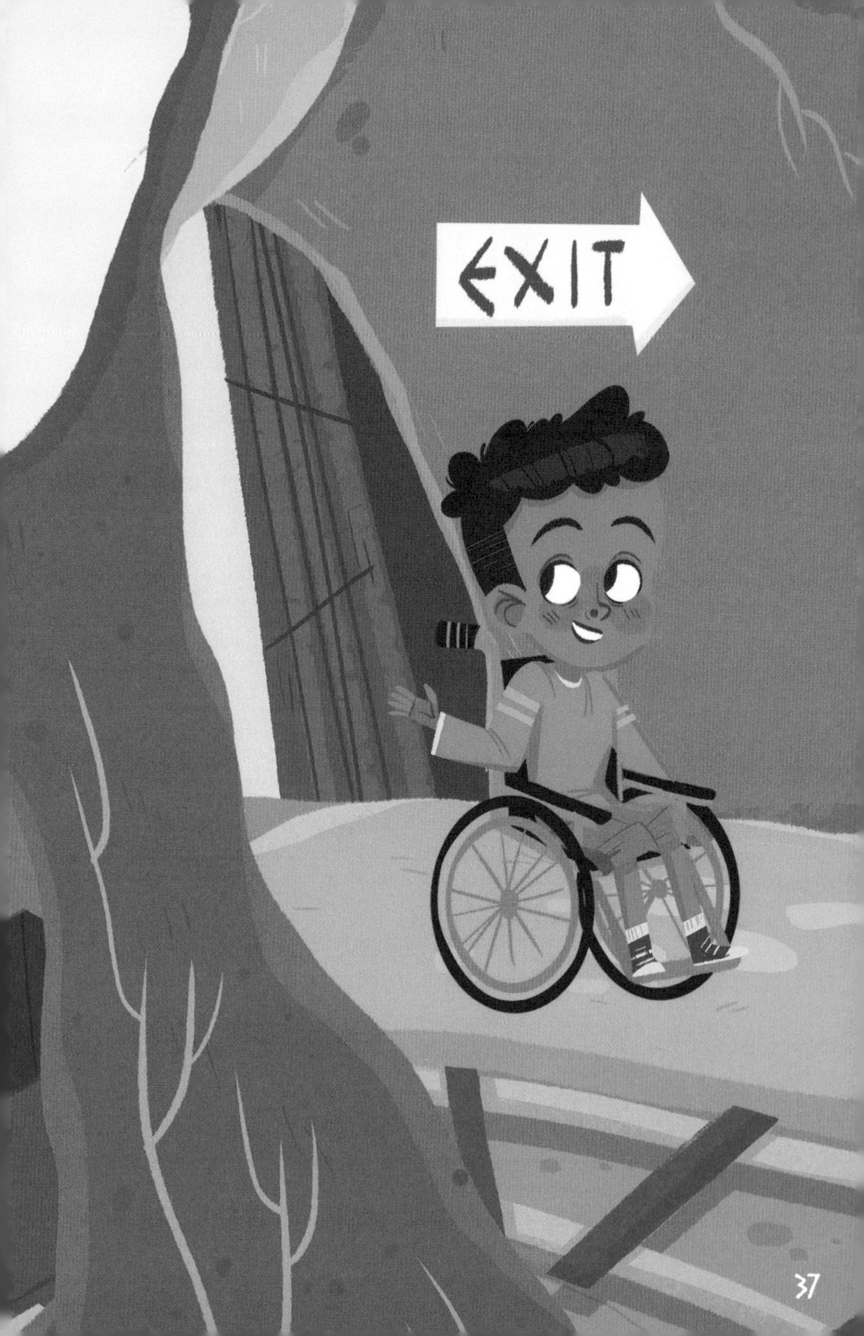
EXIT

"We LOST you in the crowd and have been LOOKING for you!" Rob says. "We thought we might find you at Pandora's Box."

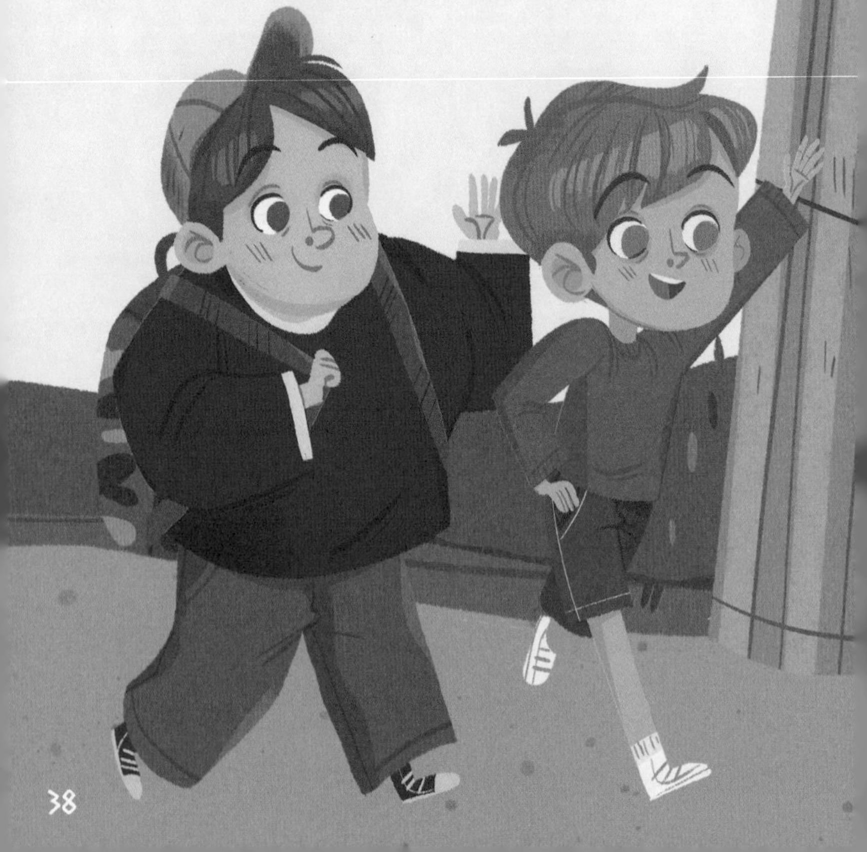

"Thanks for looking for me," Harvey says. Rob HANDS him a Fates' Funnel Cake with extra powdered sugar.

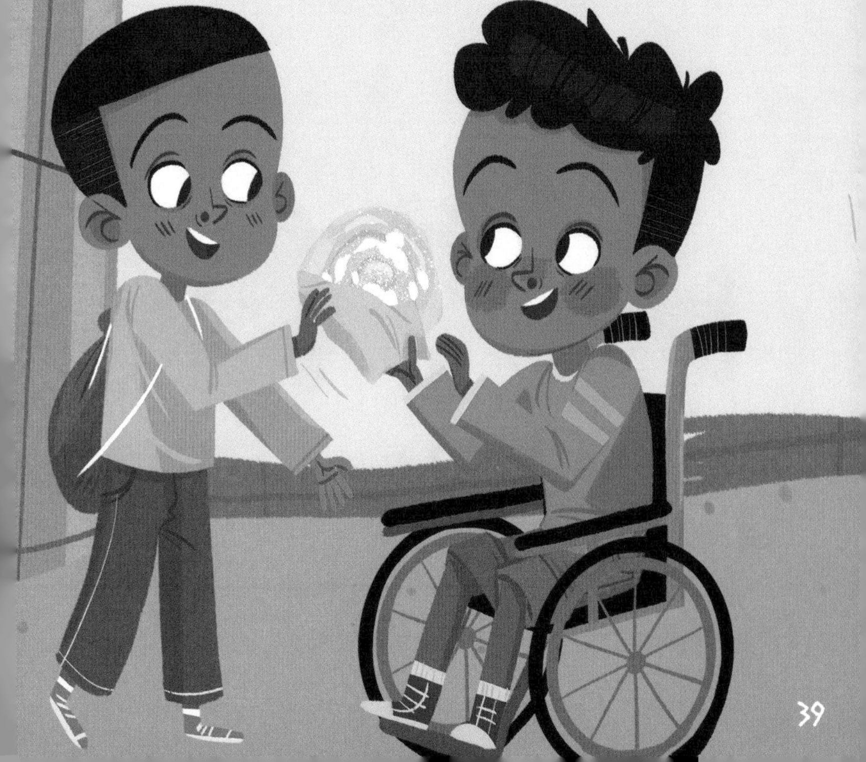

"You have to try out Prometheus's Ball of FIRE," says Rob's friend Micah.

"It's not for wheelchair users," Harvey says, SHOVING a bite of funnel cake into his mouth. "Everyone seems to forget that."

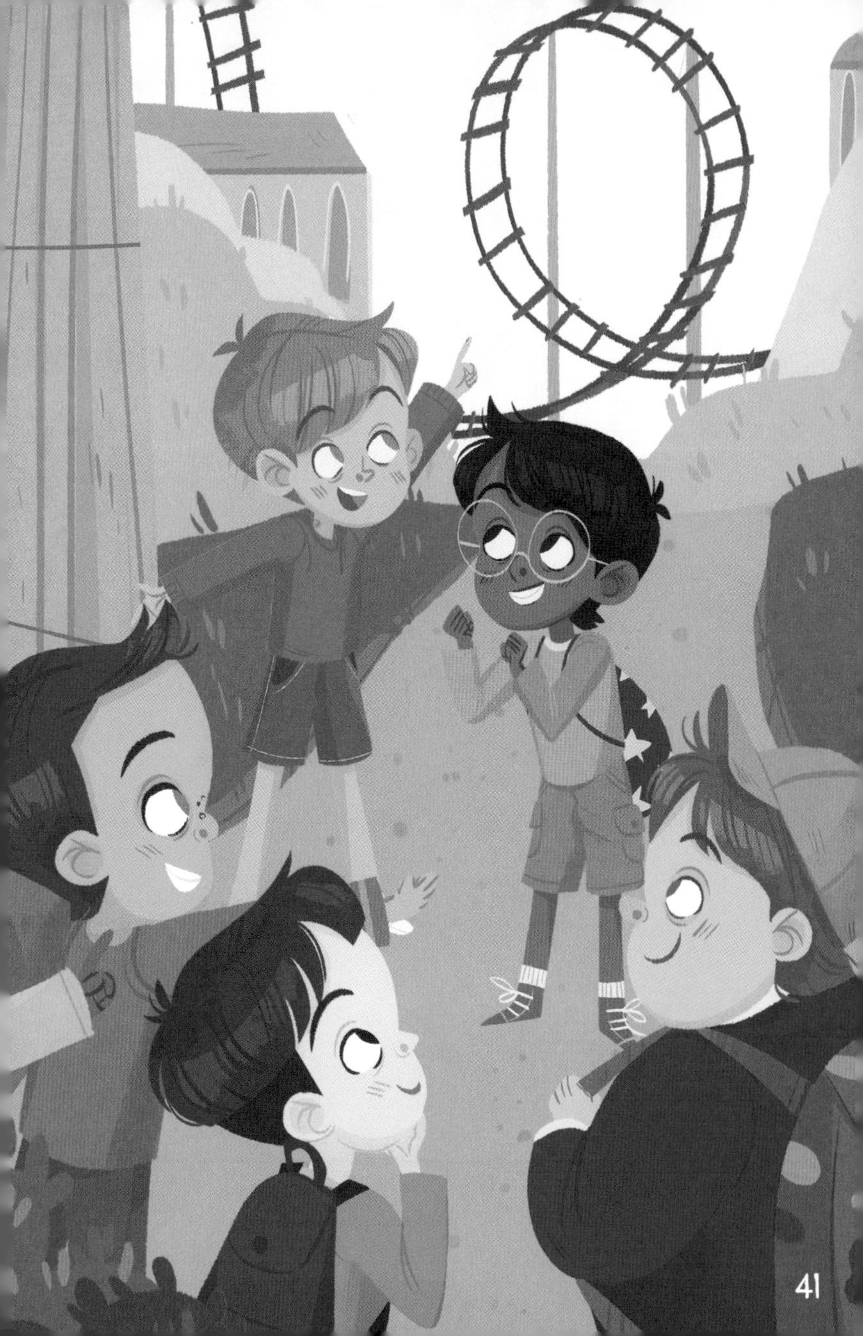

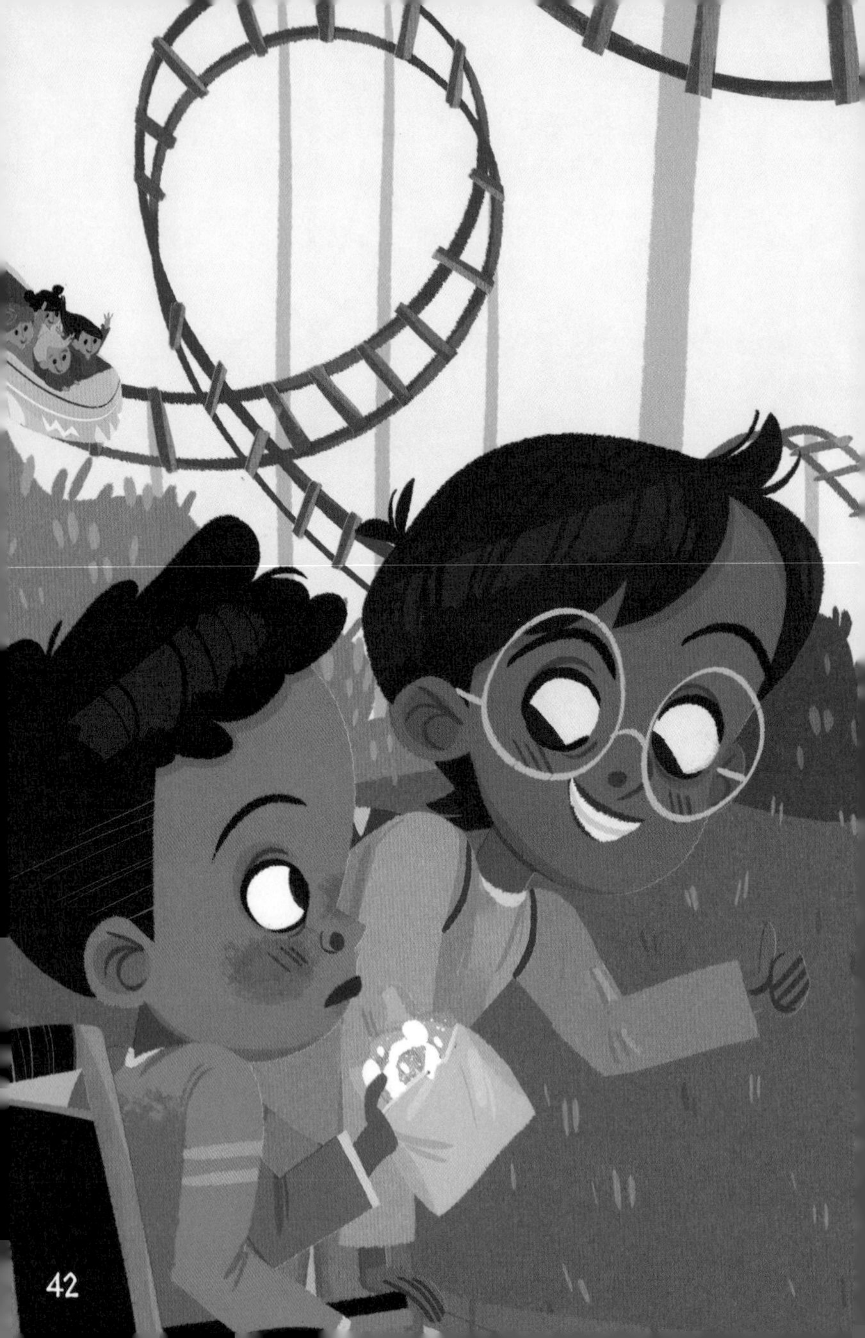

"It **TOTALLY** is for everyone," says Rob's friend Temmie. "We made a new friend. Leonora showed us how wheelchairs can go on the ride! It's so fun!"

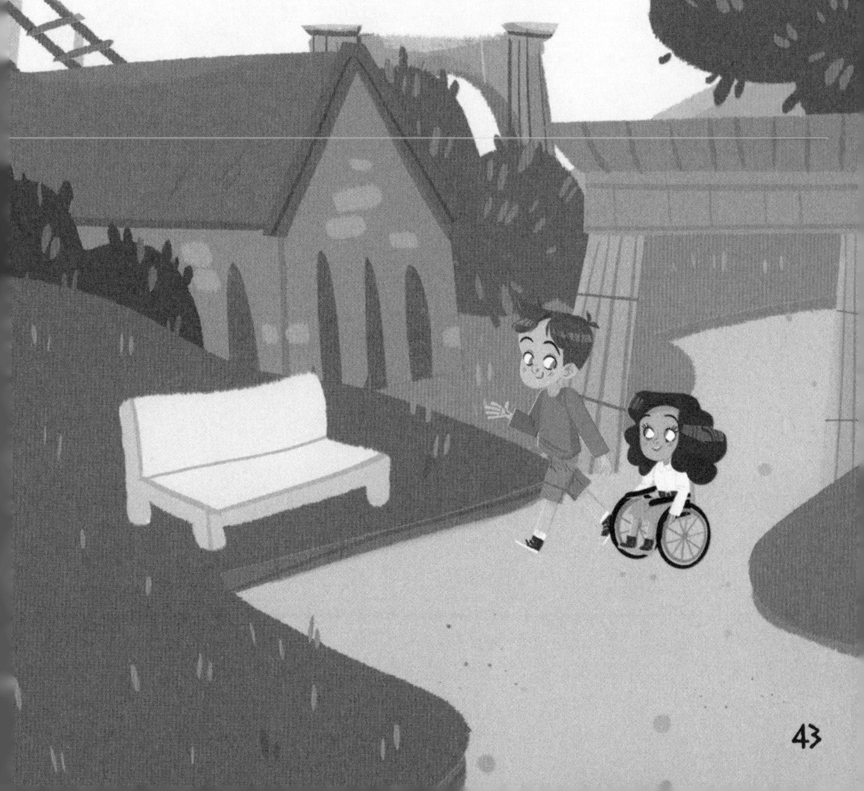

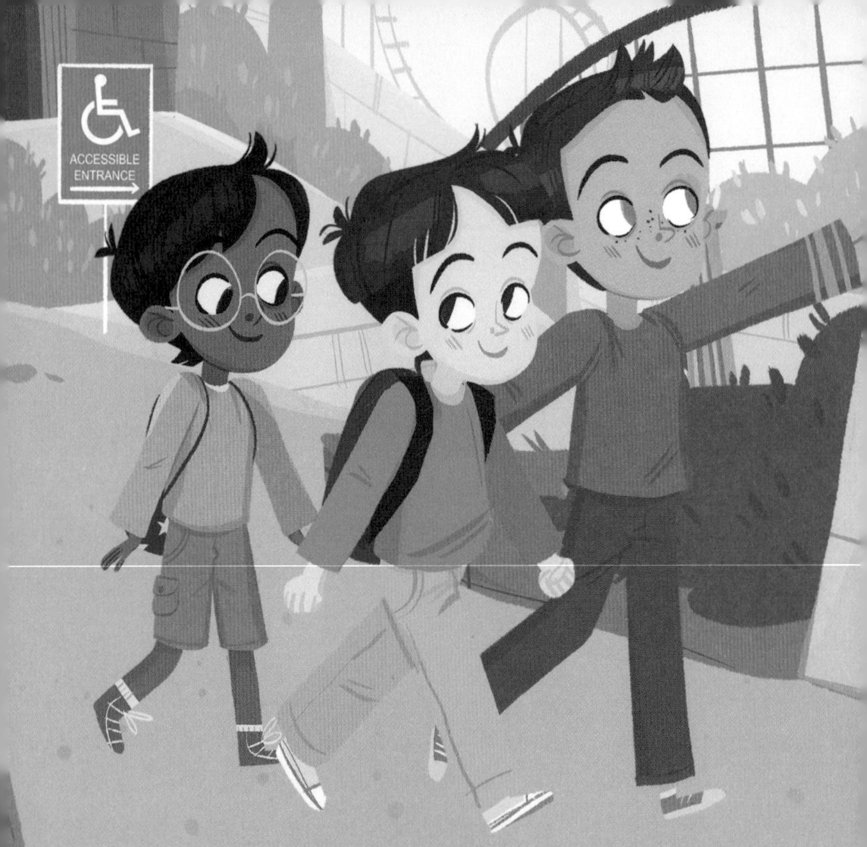
ACCESSIBLE
ENTRANCE

On the way to Prometheus's Ball of **FIRE**, Harvey notices signs that say "Accessible Entrance" **everywhere**.

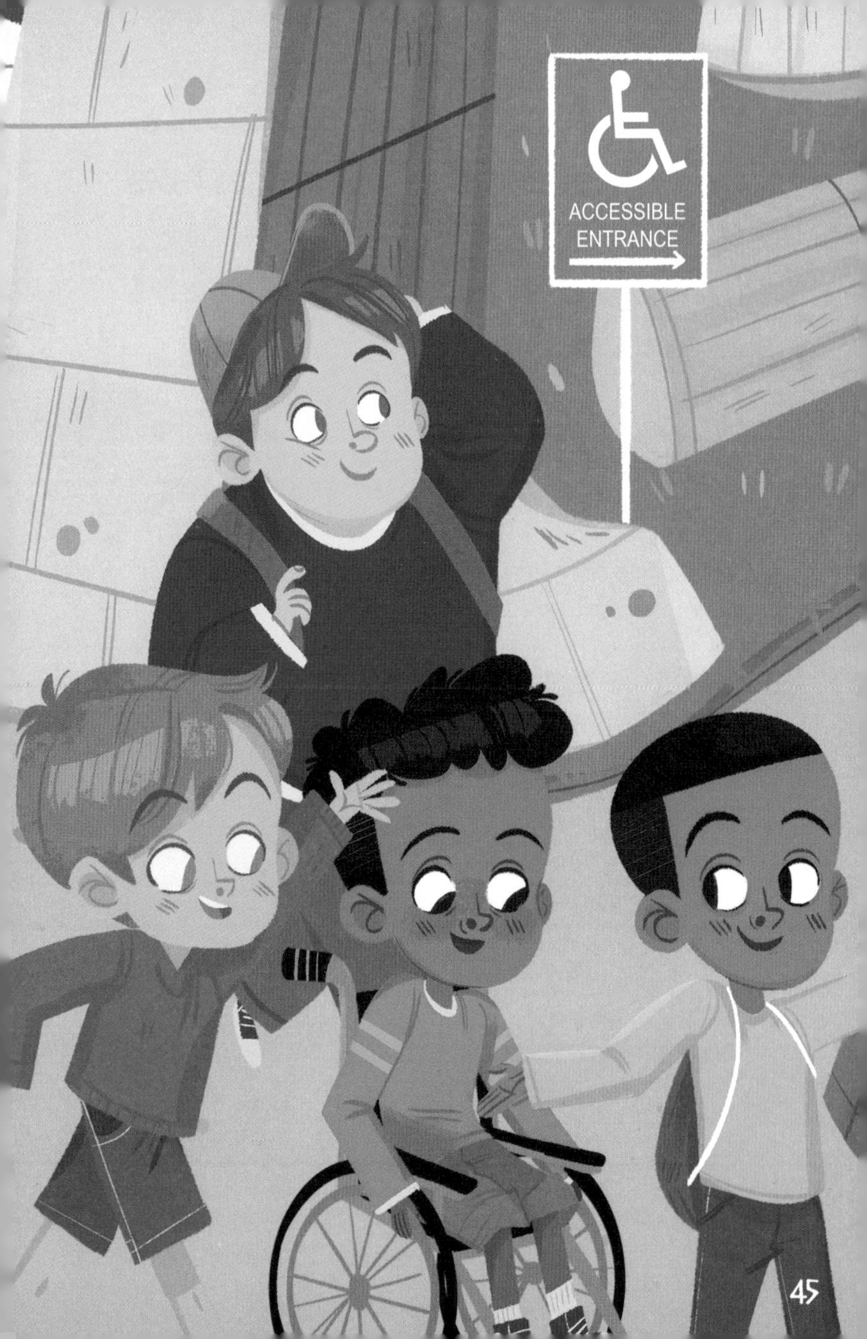
ACCESSIBLE
ENTRANCE

"Hi, Harvey," a voice says from behind him as he gets STRAPPED in. Hephaestus is on the ride too.

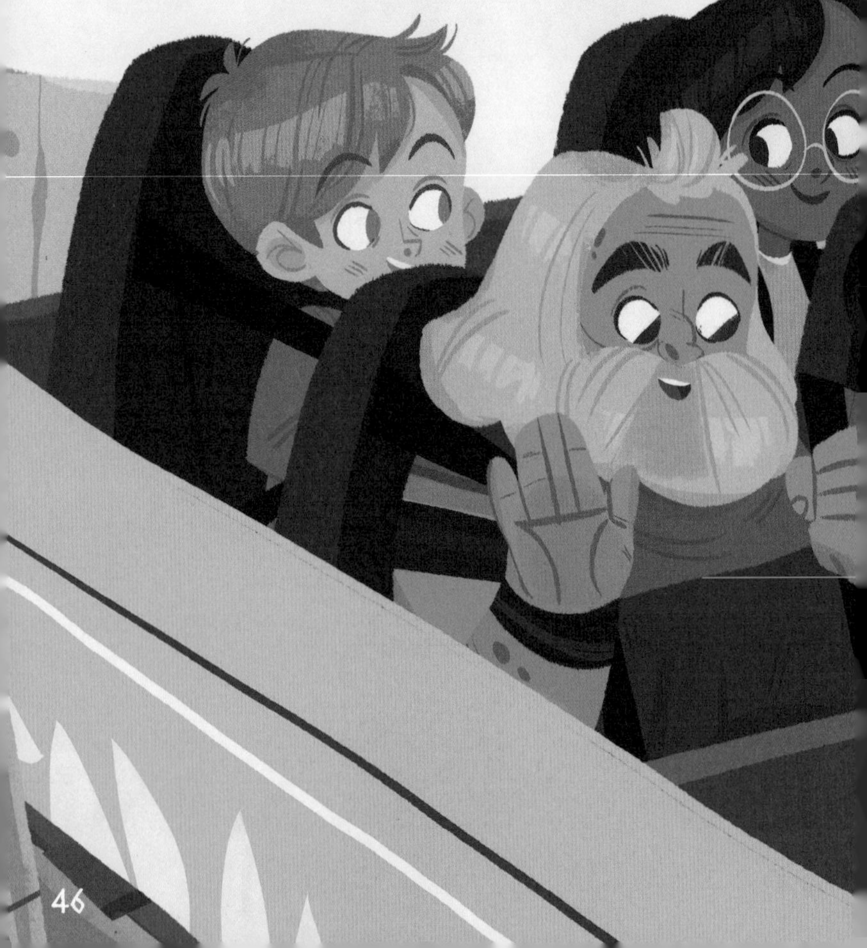

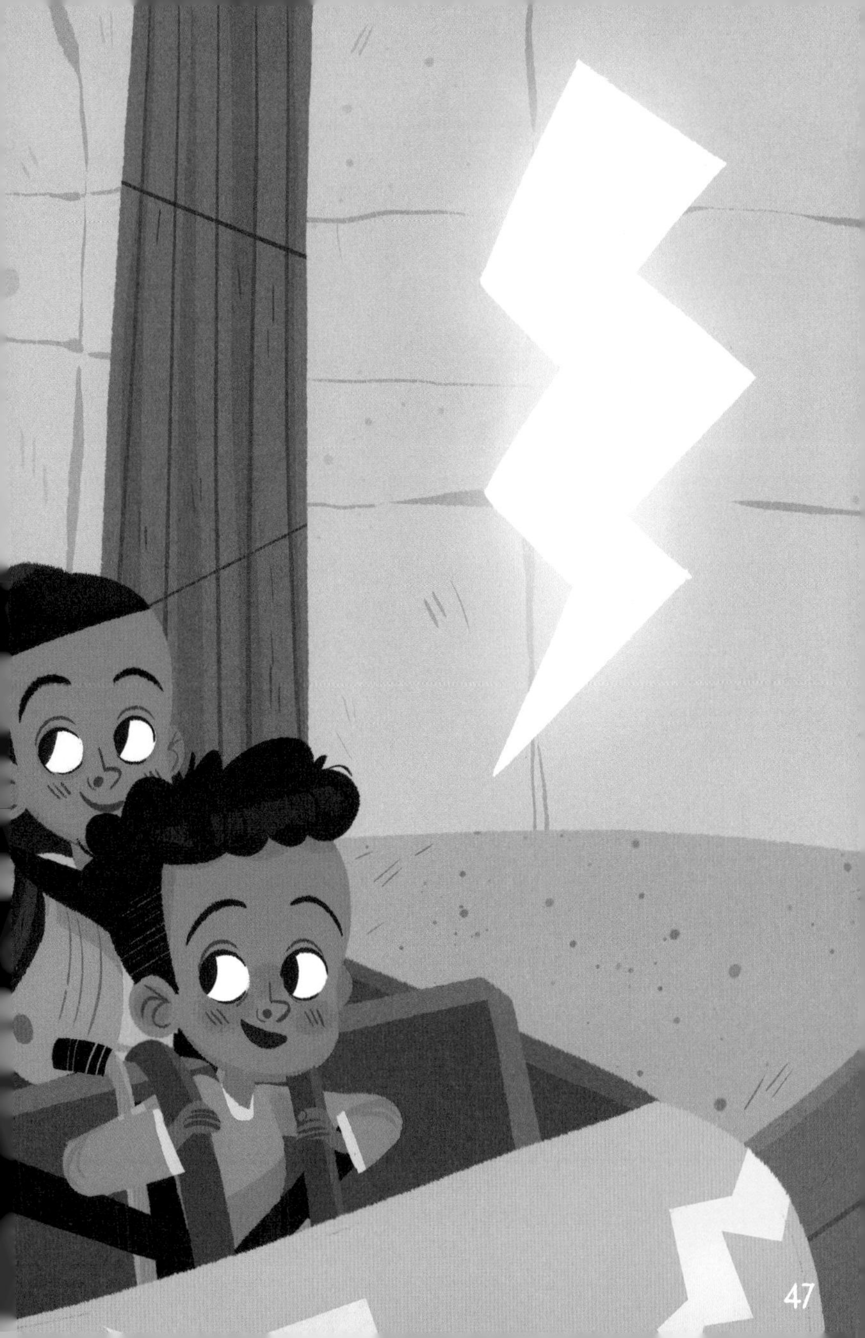

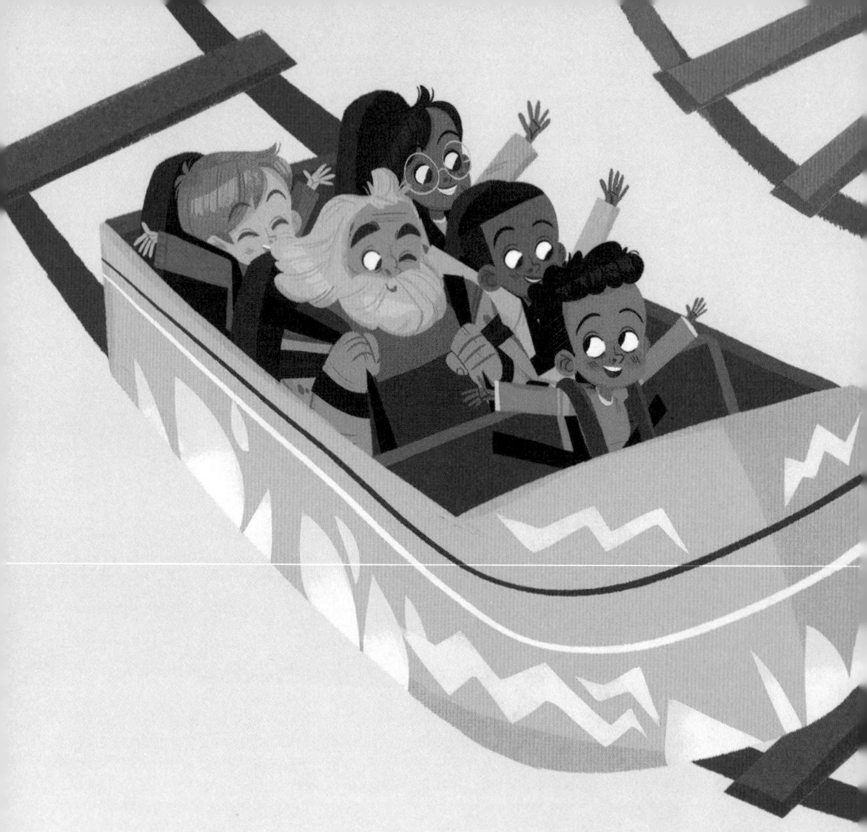

"Thank you," Hephaestus says, WINKING. "After this, can you show me more of what your smart phone can do?" he asks.